# Benny

## and

Diane Wilmer and Nicola Smee

Collins Colour Cubs

The Fair had come to Midsummer
Common and Benny couldn't stay
indoors.

He was always creeping off to watch the waltzer or sneak a ride on the dodgems.

"You mustn't come by yourself," said Bella but Benny took no notice.

He couldn't keep away from the bright lights and the loud music. He went every day, but he didn't realise he was being watched.

A man had seen him wandering
about, eating cold chips and greasy
hamburgers, and he thought Benny
was a stray.

"I'll have him!" thought the man.

One day he waited for Benny, and when he was busy gobbling up a sticky candyfloss, he crept up behind him and threw a dirty, smelly sack over his head!

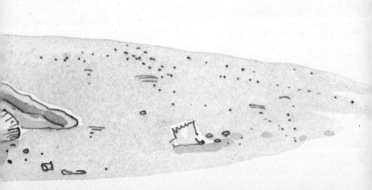

"Let me out!" howled Benny. The man threw the sack over his shoulder and ran across the Common to a house on the other side.

He locked Benny up in his shed and
kept him there all night.

"Help me, please help me!"
whined Benny, but nobody came.

Bella and Jack had spent the day searching for him. When night came they went out again with Dad.

"Benny! Benny!" they called, but their voices faded away into the big, dark sky.

By next morning they were all really
worried.

"We'll search the streets on the
other side of the Common," said
Mum.

Halfway down a small, narrow street
they heard a loud howling.
"That's Benny!" cried Bella.

They ran to the house and banged on
the door but the man wouldn't let
them in.
"We'll creep round the back," said
Mum.

When they found Benny locked up in
the shed, Mum was furious.

"If you don't give me my dog now,
I'll go straight to the police!" she
yelled.

The man quickly unlocked the shed,
and Benny rushed out.

"Take me home," he whimpered.
"Take me away from this horrible place!"

When they got back to the Common, the fair had packed up and was moving off.

"Oh! Why can't it stay forever and ever?" whined Benny.

"We'll take you to another fair," said Bella and Jack.

"Good," thought Benny. "Only this time I *won't* go there on my own."

What goes round and round and is
covered in lights?
Benny, on the Big Wheel!

ISBN 0 00 123820 5
Text © 1986 Diane Wilmer
Illustrations © 1986 Nicola Smee
The character 'Benny' © 1986 Yorkshire Television
Printed in Great Britain